USA TODAY BESTSELLING AUTHOR
MIA HARLAN

RUBBER DUCKIE *Shifter* NEXT DOOR

For the readers who wish they could spend their days as a floating bath toy.

Rubber Duckie Shifter Next Door

Mia Harlan

Chapter 1

Rachel

I march into the back yard and place my hands on my hips. "Okay, who's going to shower first?"

"Not me!" Anna, who's seven, shouts, her voice echoing across the back yard.

"Me neither." Lisa—her twin sister—scowls at me.

Noah, their five-year-old brother, copies me by placing his hands on his hips. "I'm *never* going to shower."

All three kids are absolutely adorable—dirt, grime, and all—and they remind me so much of my best friend that it hurts. They have her brown, sun-kissed hair, those familiar, piercing green eyes, and the same sprinkling of freckles on their noses. They're also a handful and a half, and they make me want to tear my hair out.

At least the twins are fraternal, so they can't pull off the old switcheroo. Lisa's taller by a full inch, and Anna's cheeks turn bright pink whenever she's upset.

I stare down at the kids and try to look tough. "You can't go to school like that. You're covered in mud, and you don't smell all that great." A definite understatement. "What will your teachers say?"

"That it's Sunday, *Rachel*," Lisa says. Smart ass.

"Yeah, *Rachel*," Noah parrots.

"There's no school on Sunday, Rachel," Anna adds, but there's no fire behind her words. Unlike her siblings, she doesn't emphasize my name in that weird way they've adopted in the last few days. Poor thing looks like she's going to cry.

I sigh. "Tomorrow's Monday. I can't send you to school like this."

Not when they haven't bathed or showered in five days. I already got a cringe-worthy lecture on personal hygiene from the principal on Friday, and a veiled threat to call Child Protective Services.

Lisa looks triumphant. "We just won't go to school until Nana's back."

She clearly thinks she's won—and maybe she has.

I almost give in. *Almost.* But if Ada's grandkids don't go to school, she'll never trust me with them again. Not when I can't even survive watching them for one week. And what if the school follows through on that threat, and the kids get taken away?

I take a deep breath. "You like school, though, don't you?"

The three of them shake their heads 'no.'

"Okay, fair enough. I never liked school either."
Shit. I shouldn't have said that.

Except that it's one hundred percent true. So how can I blame the kids for not wanting to go?

I nearly tell them exactly how much I think school sucks... until I remember that I'm the responsible adult. "There's only one week of school left before summer break. I bet you won't have any actual school work. You'll probably just watch a bunch of movies and hang out with your friends. Doesn't that sound fun?"

All three of them glare at me. *Okay then.*

I decide to switch tactics. "Don't you *want* to shower? You must be so itchy."

"We're not itchy!" Noah shouts.

The girls just shake their heads, though Anna's response is a lot less emphatic than Lisa's.

I press on. "Doesn't the smell bother you?"

Noah doesn't hesitate. "Not one bit!"

The girls take a second, but then they echo his sentiment.

Shit!

I'm way out of my element here. I don't know how to parent one kid, let alone three. And I have zero clue how to get them to do what I say.

What was Janey thinking, leaving them in my care?

I instinctively touch my right ring finger, where the gold wave-shaped ring she always wore now sits.

I should have read some parenting books before offering to watch the kids so Ada could go on her trip. I should have stuck around and helped raise them.

Noah scratches his armpit. "We're on a shower strike *forever.*"

"Noah!" Anna hisses.

Lisa glares at me. "We want Nana."

Anna's eyes fill with tears. "*Please...*"

"Oh, honey, she'll be back before you know it." I try to pull her into my arms, even though she smells more zombie than human. She backs away, tears streaming down her dirty cheeks.

Lisa scowls at me. "Now look at what you've done!"

Her words are like a slap to the face, and I suddenly feel like bawling right along with Anna.

What was I thinking, coming here? Of course, the kids don't want me around. I abandoned them when they needed me most!

I should have stuck around five years ago, after the car accident. I should have kissed their booboos, helped with homework, and tucked them in at night. But Noah was just a baby, and the twins were two, and I freaked out. So the moment Ada offered to take them in, I ran.

I was young and foolish, and I convinced myself the three of them would be better off without me. But the travel, the parties, the random hookups... none of it meant anything. The kids do. And I plan to make up for not being here. Which means either I figure this out or I throw in the towel and call their nana.

Ada would drop everything for her grandkids, no questions asked. One phone call and she'd be on the first flight home. But what if she tells me to go back to doing what I'm good at: traveling the world and having fun?

But then why did I bother studying and getting IT certified so I could find a boring, steady job? Why did I promise myself I'd be a responsible adult? Why did I spend the past year trying to convince Ada to take this trip?

I'm hyperventilating when Ada's hot-as-hell muscles-for-years neighbor peeks over the fence. "Is everything okay over there?"

"No!" all three kids shout at the same time.

I barely pay them any attention, I'm so focused on the man next door. His voice envelops me like a warm, cozy blanket and makes my spiraling thoughts short-circuit.

He's got that just-rolled-out-of-bed look that makes me wish I'd been rolling in it with him. His dirty blond hair is in desperate need of a comb and a cut, but I'm willing to tackle anyone who comes at it with a brush or scissors. Or go to beauty school for the chance to run my fingers through it myself.

He's only visible from the chest-up, but the fence is tall, which means so is he. Is it bad that a part of me is hoping he's naked from the waist down? Yes. That is bad. And weird and wrong, and I'm definitely not imagining long, tanned legs and a hard...

Stop it, Rachel! Not in front of the kids!

Don't picture him taking off his blue polo shirt to reveal huge, delicious pecs that are just begging to be licked. No, don't! Stop. Stop. Stop!

My eyes snap up to his face—*look at me being all PG*—and oh boy, that face is as gorgeous as the rest of him. His angular jaw, covered in stubble, and those twinkling blue eyes do something funny to my insides. And when his lips curve up into a slow smile, I'm gone.

My belly does somersaults. My heart rate accelerates. My womb shouts 'breed me' when it should be running for the hills.

After the week I've just had, having *more* kids is not the answer. Not even with *him*.

Chapter 2

Rachel

Ada's glorious neighbor gives me a once-over, and heat floods my cheeks.

I give myself a mental slap on the wrist. *Bad, bad, Rachel.*

Men are off-limits. I swore them off when I promised myself I'd be a responsible adult. I can't go back on that promise with the first hottie I see. Even if he is absolutely drool-worthy.

I lick my lips.

I bet women do that all the time when they see him, but he still seems concerned. "Are you okay?" he asks me.

"No, she's not!" Lisa shouts. "And neither are we!"

At least we can agree on something. I sigh.

I just licked my lips at a stranger while standing in the back yard surrounded by stinky kids.

I grimace. "I need help."

I really do, even if it's not the 'sweep me off my feet and get me naked' kind.

I don't usually offload on hot strangers, but it's that or lock myself in the guest bedroom and bawl my eyes out. And that's clearly not an option.

"No, we need help," Lisa snaps. "She stole our nana."

I gape at her.

Anna nods emphatically, and her tears turn to loud sobs, while Noah scowls at me like I'm some kidnapper.

"I didn't steal their nana." I rush to explain before Mr. Piercing-Blue-Eyes-Next-Door calls CPS, or worse, the police. "She's on a cruise, and I'm watching the kids until she's back. I'm their godmother."

"She's lying," Lisa snaps.

"No, I'm not. I swear. I really am their godmother." I instinctively reach for Janey's ring and trace its wavelike shape. "You can ask Ada." I hope he knows Ada. What if he's the sort of next-door neighbor who keeps to himself? "You have to believe me!"

"Of course I believe you." He chuckles. "You must be Rachel. Ada told me a lot about you."

My shoulders sag in relief, and I let go of the ring. "All good things, I hope?"

"Bad things," Noah snaps.

"Really bad," Lisa adds.

Anna nods.

I'm inclined to believe them.

Chances are Ada told him I'm flighty, irresponsible, and I abandoned Janey's kids when they needed me most.

"Of course they were all good things," Mr. Bulging Biceps says politely.

I try not to stare at his muscles. They stretch the short sleeves of his polo as he casually rests an arm on top of the fence and watches me with those piercing baby blues.

I flush.

"Ada asked me to check in on you from time to time."

Yup, she *definitely* told him I'm irresponsible.

He shoots me a winning smile. "I'm Sig."

"He lives next door," Anna says, stating the obvious.

Lisa places her hands on her hips. "Sig's friends with Nana."

"Sig," I repeat, wondering if it's short for Sigmund. Before I can ask, he turns to the kids.

"So, what's going on, you guys? I heard a lot of shouting."

I answer the question before they can accuse me of nana-napping again. "The kids are refusing to shower, but they've got school tomorrow. They can't go looking like this."

"Shower?" He frowns. "Well, that's your first mistake."

Maybe their smell doesn't reach the fence. "They really need one."

"Showers are for chumps. What they need is a bath."

Did I take baths instead of showers at their age? Could it be that easy? I turn to the kids and pray that he's right. "How about a bath, then?"

"No," Lisa says.

I glance at Anna and Noah hopefully. They shake their heads.

I hold in a frustrated sigh. "Look, I get that I'm not Nana. And that you miss her. And that I have no clue what I'm doing here. But can we please just make the best of it? We can order pizza with pineapple tonight." We did that on Monday, back when the kids still thought of me as their fun godmother who sends them expensive gifts on birthdays and holidays to assuage her guilt for not being there.

"I love pizza with pineapple," Noah says wistfully.

Lisa shakes her head. "You can't bribe us with pizza. Nana will get us all the pizza we want when she's back."

That doesn't sound like Ada—who's responsibility personified—but Noah nods. "Nana loves pineapple. She has good taste."

"I like pineapple, too," I lie. *Pineapple does not belong on pizza!*

All three kids glare at me, and I shoot Sig a 'help me' look.

He mouths something, and since my eyes are already glued to his lips, I'm pretty sure he's saying "I've got this." Or maybe it's "stop, please." Hell, for all I know, he just mouthed "I love bees."

I raise an eyebrow, hoping to hell it's door number one. Bees wouldn't be much help in this situation... unless he's trying to tell me "you catch more flies with honey than vinegar." Which won't help. Trust me. I tried sucking up to the kids, and it does not work. At all.

"I have an idea." Sig shoots me a slow smile that makes my toes curl. "Who wants to go swimming?"

"I do," Noah shouts.

Anna seems to instantly perk up, but Lisa hesitates. "Are you coming, Sig?"

He nods and turns to me. "Rachel, why don't you pack some swimsuits and clean clothes and meet me out front in ten?"

I hesitate. Wouldn't it be irresponsible to go somewhere with a complete stranger? But the kids obviously know him. And if I don't, there's no way in hell I'm getting these kids to school tomorrow. Ada will have definitive proof I'm irresponsible, and the school might even call CPS, and... and...

Sig knows Ada and the kids, I remind myself. *And it's not like I have a better solution.*

"Sounds like a plan."

I head into the house and run around like a madwoman, getting us packed in record time. No way am I giving the kids a chance to change their minds.

When I come back outside, the kids are playing a game of catch, and there's no sign of Sig. And unlike him, I'm too short to peek over the shared fence, so I'm forced to walk around to the other side.

When I enter his back yard, I find him sitting on his porch, his back to me, his phone glued to his ear.

"Sig!" I call out.

He jumps. And disappears. As in, vanishes into thin air. *Bam!*

His phone tumbles down the porch steps and lands face-down on the grass.

On the other side of the fence, things get suspiciously quiet. I need to go check on the kids, but I'm too busy gaping at the rubber duckie sitting on the porch where Sig was seconds ago.

What the actual fu...dge sticks? And look at me, censoring my thoughts like a good guardian!

I've gone insane, haven't I?

I blink a few times.

Sig was just there! I swear he was. Wasn't he? Deep breaths, Rachel!

I close my eyes and open them again. I don't know what to expect to happen. For Sig to re-appear right where he was? For the phone and duckie to disappear, so I can convince myself I imagined the whole thing?

I can still picture him right there, his broad shoulders stretching his blue short-sleeved polo, his arm muscles bulging as he holds his phone up to his ear. *He was right there. I swear he was.*

Of course he wasn't! Not unless there's an alien running around town with a ray gun that turns people into bath toys.

And just like that, it all clicks.

Kids really can drive you crazy sometimes. As in literally insane. Because a hallucination... is the only reasonable explanation...

And the fact that it rhymes must mean I'm certifiable.

Chapter 3

Sig

I stare at Rachel from my vantage point on the porch steps. *This cannot be happening...*

Except it is.

I grimace. Internally, that is. Externally, I'm a quacking rubber duck. Not literally quacking. I can't quack or talk in duckie form, and if I could, chances are I'd squeak. But until I shift back, I'm stuck in one spot, staring up at the beautiful, hyperventilating woman across the yard.

When I saw Rachel in Ada's yard earlier, she looked cute in an I-just-got-out-of-bed sort of way. If it weren't for the kids, I would have tried to seduce her out of her plaid pink pajama pants and white t-shirt. Then I would have wrapped my hand around her blonde ponytail and...

Pull your head out of the gutter, Duck!

I may not be able to spring a rubber boner, but this is still not the time. I need to focus on shifting back. But how am I supposed to focus on anything when the woman's wearing shorts and a tank top that hug her tall, slim frame?

A tanned patch of skin peeks out just above her waistband, and my fingers itch with the need to touch her. Figure of speech, of course, since I'm in duckie form. But the need to drag Rachel upstairs and yank her pants down is driving me insane.

Fuck a duck, I've got it bad.

And poor Rachel has got it bad in an entirely different way. She's hyperventilating, her beautiful hazel eyes are wide, and she's gaping at me like she's never seen a man shift into a rubber duck before.

Of course she hasn't. She's human!

She closes her eyes, opens them, closes them, opens them... over and over again, as though that will somehow change reality. And when it doesn't, she spins around and races out of my yard.

Shift back, shift back, shift back!

I need to go after her before she packs the kids into Ada's van and drives away without me.

Shift back, shift back, shift back!

It always takes forever after I'm startled, and this time is no different.

It feels like an eternity before I finally do. The magic returns me to my human form along with my clothes, so all that's left is to grab my phone, shoot off a quick text, and go after her.

To my relief, I find her sitting on her back porch. But her head is between her knees and the kids are watching her with matching triumphant looks.

I need to do something about that, too, but one problem at a time.

"Rachel?" I say her name softly, then kneel in front of her.

"Sig..." She stares at me, eyes wide. I wait for the questions, but she blinks a few times and shoots me a tentative smile. "Ready to go?"

So that's how we're going to play it? Just ignore the giant rubber duckie in the room and pretend nothing happened?

What ever happened to if it looks like a duck, swims like a duck, and quacks like a duck, then it's probably a duck?

I sigh. "Yes, I'm all set."

"Great." Rachel claps her hands. "Okay, everyone, let's go."

Lisa glares at her with more malice than a seven-year-old has any right to feel and shouts, "You can't come!"

Noah crosses his arms in front of his chest. "We don't want you."

Anna, whose cheeks are streaked with tears, whimpers. "We want Nana."

If Ada hadn't told me about Rachel before she left for her trip, I'd be worried. And probably making phone calls to make sure she should really be here. Instead, I'm confused. How did she manage to turn Ada's sweet, polite grandkids into little rebels?

I've been too busy with work to pay attention to things on the other side of the fence, but Rachel's barely been here a few days. She can't possibly be as bad as the kids clearly seem to think. Yes, she prefers showers to baths, but I'm willing to bet I can change her mind. Later... First, she needs my help, and I'm going to figure out what's going on with the kids and how to fix it.

The most likely explanation? They're homesick. Or Nana-sick, since this is their home and Ada's the one who left. But shouldn't they just be a little mopey and not openly hostile?

Is Rachel mistreating them?

As soon as the thought crosses my mind, I push it away. I know deep down that she's not. If I were human, I'd ask a few questions, to be sure. But I don't need to do that, I just know. I knew from the moment our eyes met, and I'm going to help her and the kids in any way I can.

"I've got a surprise for you, kids," I announce.

"What is it?" Noah perks up. Now we're talking.

I gesture for him to come closer. The girls follow.

One whiff of their 'unique' scent, and my heart goes out to poor, poor Rachel. How is she not wearing a nose plug? If I had to smell them all day, I'd jump out the window. The house is a bungalow, so I'm not even being dramatic.

Despite my better judgment, I lean in closer and quickly whisper my plan. I hope it works, because impressing Rachel is the number one item on my to-do list. And this is coming from a guy whose only focus for the past year has been launching his own business.

The moment I'm done explaining, Noah takes off across the back yard yelling, "Race you to the car!"

The girls squeal and give chase. They're taller and faster and easily outpace him. You can never win when you have older sisters.

Rachel stares after them, mouth agape. Her lips look soft and kissable, and oh, so tempting. I try to resist. Fuck a duck, I try. It's too soon. I'm moving too fast. I'm going to scare her off.

I take a step back, and another, but then she looks at me and I'm gone. When her gaze drops to my lips, I know I have to taste my fated mate. Now.

Her eyes widen as I cross the distance between us and grab her sexy ponytail. She gasps, and I cover her lips in a heated kiss.

I half-expect her to slap me and tell me to take a hike. Instead, she melts into me like she needs this as much as I do.

A soft moan slips past her lips, and my cock strains against the zipper of my shorts. She tastes like strawberries—and now I'll get hard every time I have a bagel. Strawberry cream cheese, my fridge, top shelf. Don't knock it until you try it.

I slide one hand down Rachel's back, to that bare patch of skin at her waist, and groan as my fingers graze her warm skin. She feels so good in my arms. So ducking perfect!

And our first kiss? Forget sparks. The entire world explodes in bursts of color, because kissing Rachel is *everything*.

"Rachel. Sig. Hurry up!" Lisa—the bossy sister—shouts from the front of the house.

Duck a duckity duck!

Rachel instantly pulls away from me. Her lips are swollen from our kiss, her breath comes out in pants, and her eyes are wide and slightly spooked. She's also twirling her ring around and around her ring finger. Her *right* ring finger, not left, though my gut tells me she'd never have kissed me like that if she were taken.

But she shakes her head. "I can't."

I know it, deep down, that she doesn't just mean right now. She means ever. She's going to deny the chemistry between us and pull away.

Don't ask me how I know, but I do, and I can't let that happen. I can't let her put up a wall between us. Because from the moment our eyes met over that fence, I knew Rachel was mine. I staked a claim on her before I got a taste of how good we could be together, and I'm never letting her go.

Chapter 4

Sig

I grab the duffle bag at Rachel's feet and head towards the car at a fast clip. "Let's go."

She races after me. "Coming."

You're not yet, but if I have it my way... I groan and speed up. No way in hell am I going there... or giving her a chance to change her mind about this trip. Not when it's an opportunity for me to spend more time with her. "Come on. The kids need you."

"The kids! Fuck!" She races after me. "I mean fudge."

"Duck," I suggest my go-to swear.

"D-duck?"

I wish I knew what was going on in that pretty head of hers. Is she trying to convince herself she didn't see me shift? Does she think she imagined the whole thing?

"Duck is easier to remember than fudge," I tell her.

"Right. Duck." She hurries around me and races up to the kids. "Sorry we took so long."

All three of them glare at her.

It's obvious that she cares about the kids, even when they're making her life a living hell. Makes me picture us having kids of our own—another three, to bring our family up to eight. Well, nine, if you count Nana, and I certainly do. She practically adopted me the moment I moved in next door, baking me cookies, asking about my business, encouraging me to share my passion with the world.

But I'm getting ahead of myself. I can't ask Rachel to marry me when we just met. She's still in complete denial... not just about my duckie status, but about *us*.

I've got all day to get through to her, and I have a plan.

I grab her hand, marveling at how perfect it feels in mine, and pull her toward Ada's van. "Can you drive?"

I've never learned, and with good reason. I could never get behind the wheel knowing that if something were to startle me, I could shift. Sure, I'd just bounce off the car walls, but what about other people on the road? They could get seriously hurt!

Rachel pulls out the car keys and manually unlocks the old Dodge. I wait for it to stall, but the engine's smooth as butter. And the smell wafting from the kids is equivalent to the dump off Carlton Avenue... which makes me wonder if they've been rolling in garbage.

I roll down my windows—literally... because the car is that old. I turn the ducking crank handle as fast as it will go, while the window slides down at a crawl. Rachel copies me. I'd say it's proof that we're on the same wavelength, but the kids roll their windows down too, eager to escape the smell. Because. It. Is. That. Bad.

Rachel sets her phone on the car mount, and I program the GPS. She barely has a chance to pull out of the driveway when Noah asks. "Are we there yet?"

I grin, and so does Rachel. Definitely on the same wavelength.

"Fifteen minutes," I say as my gaze slides down to her legs. They're long, lean, and tanned.

"Do you like swimming?" I ask.

"Yes!" all three kids shout from the back.

Rachel turns to gape at me. "How'd you do that?"

"Do what?"

"Convince them to..." She lowers her voice. "Go swimming."

I chuckle. "I have my secrets."

She smiles, glances at the GPS, and merges onto the highway.

Noah claps his hands. "We're going to Rubber Duckie World!"

I sigh. "We gotta work on keeping secrets, bud."

"Sorry, Sig!"

Rachel gives me the most adorable frown, and I wish I could kiss it away. "What's Rubber Duckie World?"

"Only the best place ever!" Noah yells.

I chuckle. "I appreciate the vote of confidence, but you haven't even tried it yet." Though I have been stopping by Ada's house with progress updates and photos, so the kids know everything there is to know about the place. I turn to Rachel. "It's not open to the public yet."

Rachel frowns. "Then how are we going to get in?"

"Sig owns it. Duh," Lisa says. Girl's got some attitude on her, and she's clearly not on Team Rachel. I plan to get to the bottom of why, and fix it, before the day is done.

For now, I turn to Rachel. "The grand opening is next weekend."

She's still frowning. "What is it, exactly?"

I place a hand on my heart with a dramatic gasp. "How have you not heard of Rubber Duckie World?"

I'm mostly teasing, though I am a bit surprised. My water park is the talk of the town, and the behind-the-scenes footage I've released has been featured in magazines and viral videos for months. The grand opening is completely sold out, and so is the August summer festival, not to mention that I've sold ten times more season passes and VIP memberships than I'd hoped—all before we even opened the gates.

But Rachel just shakes her head, sending her blonde ponytail flying. Strands of hair graze tanned, muscular shoulders, and I picture it down—sliding across her bare shoulders while she rides my cock.

I swallow and force myself to look away. *Breathe, duck!*

"Is anyone going to tell me what Rubber Duckie World is or not?" Rachel whines.

"It's a water park with over a dozen—" I start.

"It's got massive slides!" Lisa shouts, practically bouncing in her seat.

"And a pool with bubbles," Anna adds softly. "And all these rubber ducks."

"The Duckie Tub," I clarify.

"And you can ride ducks like horses," Noah shouts.

"Down the lazy river," I add. "Ducks are better than tubes." Which is a known fact. Not much else needs to be said.

"They are," Anna says. Kid's got good taste.

"Can we see the gift shop?" Lisa asks. "I want to get Nana a grandma rubber duckie. I'm going to give it to her when she comes back."

"Sure thing." I glance over my shoulder at her and catch her glaring at the back of Rachel's seat. Time to deflect. "I've got some grandma duckies knitting sweaters in stock. I'm still waiting for grandma duckies drinking coffee to come in."

"Nana loves to knit," Noah says.

I guess that's settled.

Rachel shoots me this adorably confused look as she takes the exit I programmed into her GPS. I'm used to that reaction, since most people haven't heard of rubber duck collectors—but my water park is going to change all that.

"Are you sure it's okay that we're going before it's even open?" Rachel asks.

"Yes," Lisa shouts.

I chuckle. "We're shooting some publicity videos later today, so all the rides are operational. My friend, Reaper, is meeting us there. He runs the Duckie Diner, and he's a certified lifeguard. Everyone on staff is, and a few others will be there to run the rides."

I don't add how much I'm paying them for that last minute favor.

Rachel smiles. "Thanks so much for having us, Sig. You don't know how much I appreciate it."

I'd do anything for Rachel. I just don't want to come on too strong and scare her off by telling her. So instead, I respond with a breezy, "It's no trouble at all."

She smiles softly. "I promise we won't stay long."

All three kids—and one grown-ass man—groan. Because, if I have it my way, Rachel and the kids are staying forever. Nana, too.

We're meant to be.

I just need to convince Rachel of that... and it looks like I have my work cut out for me.

Chapter 5

Rachel

Sig claps his hands. "Are you ready to be the first kids to ever set foot inside Rubber Duckie World?"

Noah claps and cheers. Lisa lets out a whoop. Anna jumps up and down.

Me? I'm frozen in place, my gaze drawn to the two giant rubber duckies sitting on either side of the gate.

They look just like the one from this morning's hallucination. I can still picture Sig sitting on his front porch, light blue polo hugging huge biceps, until poof. Gone. And then the sound of his phone tumbling down the porch steps. And the duckie left in his place.

I swear it happened… but I know for a fact it didn't. People don't just turn into rubber ducks…

"This way," Sig calls as he leads the way toward the front gate.

I force my feet to follow. Duckies or not, we're going in. And not just because the kids need to be submerged in water, stat.

Moment of truth? I *love* water parks!

I want to go on all the rides, especially Quack Attack—the giant slide Sig pointed out when we first drove up. It towers over the other attractions, and I can practically hear it calling my name.

Ride me, Rachel. Quack.

I shake my head. I'm a responsible adult who is only here to make sure the kids get cleaned up and ready for school tomorrow.

That's the only reason I'm excited.

I just about manage to convince myself of it by the time Sig's friend, Reaper, unlocks the gate and ushers us inside. "Follow me for the grand tour. And remember, no running."

With a name like Reaper, I expect a scary-looking biker with a gazillion tattoos. And he is burly, but definitely not frightening. Hard to be when you're dressed in bright yellow board shorts and a matching tank. He's also got a friendly smile, and he's an attractive man, but he's got nothing on Sig.

My neighbor—well, Ada's neighbor—threads his fingers through mine as we follow Reaper and the kids down the paved path. I know I should pull away, but I can't bring myself to. I like having his large hand wrapped around mine. He makes me feel safe, and more than a bit turned on. That kiss...

Don't think about the kiss, Rachel. Because if I think about it, I'll want to kiss him again, and I can't. Not if I'm going to prove to Ada that I'm a responsible adult.

Why is that getting harder and harder by the second?

Noah lets out a whoop and races ahead.

"This place is amazing!" Lisa shouts, giving chase.

Anna races after her twin. I'm about to shout for the kids to slow down when Reaper blows the whistle hanging around his neck.

The kids spin around. Their bright, sunny faces are an in-my-face reminder of just how miserable they've been these last few days.

I'm a terrible guardian. They deserve better.

The worst part is that we've always gotten along. But that was when I visited for the occasional birthday or Christmas dinner. The kids like me in small doses. They were even happy for the first few days after Ada left. And then, they had enough of me.

It's all my fault. I should have started with monthly visits, or every other weekend. My dad did that, and it worked out. Well, minus the part where he'd forget me at the grocery store or the mall from time to time.

Still... scheduled visits are a good place to start. Assuming that after this train wreck of a week, Ada lets me anywhere near the kids.

Get your act together, Rachel.

I discreetly remove my hand from Sig's and take in the sprawling water park. "You really built this entire place?"

He nods. "Do you like it?"

I spin around full circle. "It's *amazing*!"

And I'm not lying. The place is huge, and each ride looks better than the last. Even the duckies make me smile despite this morning's incident. Not to mention the kids are finally happy. What more could I ask for?

Sig grins. "Opening Rubber Duckie World was my dream since I was a kid! Grandad was a duckie collector. He had hundreds in his basement, but to me, it always felt like duckie prison." He rubs the back of his neck. "A collection like that shouldn't be hidden away. It's meant to be admired. So I promised myself that one day, I'd build a place where all the duckies could be free."

His cheeks take on an endearing flush, and I resist the urge to kiss him.

"You did way better than a basement," I tell him honestly. "These are some lucky duckies."

Sig grins. "And you are going to love this next part." He leads us toward the changing rooms and turns to the kids. "What's the number one rule of Rubber Duckie World?"

They look stumped. I am too.

"Everyone has to shower before they're allowed on any of the rides."

I wait for the kids to argue, but they cheer. *They actually cheer!*

If I knew all it took to get them cleaned up was taking them to a water park... I'd have been hard out of luck.

Sig turns to me and lowers his voice. "Normally, I'm firmly Team Bath, but we had to take sanitation, water usage, efficiency, and accessibility under consideration, and it just wasn't workable for the public change rooms."

He sounds apologetic, like it's a major sticking point.

"Showers do make more sense," I whisper back.

We head inside, change into bathing suits, and hit the showers. I expect something boring and functional, but water flows out of large, cheerful rubber duck bills. The kids have a great time. They even let me help them scrub off some of the grime.

By the time we're ready to go, a few other Rubber Duckie World employees—all dressed in bright yellow—join us.

Sig claps his hands. I try to ignore how delicious he looks in yellow board shorts and matching flip flops. "Which ride do you want to go on first?"

"Quack Attack!" I shout, then remember that I'm supposed to act like a responsible—boring—adult. And that I really need to stop ogling the man. "I mean... why don't we let the kids decide..."

They start pointing in various directions, shouting descriptions of rides, and getting progressively louder and louder.

Before the situation can get out of hand, Reaper blows his whistle. The kids instantly fall silent.

Sig clears his throat, and I try not to stare at his lips as he speaks. "I recommend starting with a few of the smaller slides first and working our way up. Who wants to try the Duckie Drift?"

It turns out to be a lazy river filled with rubber duckies. We even get adorable duckie-shaped floaties, and Sig helps the kids count duckies as we drift past.

One duckie, two duckie, yellow duckie, blue duckie. Pink duckie, green duckie, king duckie, queen duckie.

We're happy and relaxed by the time we reach the other end. And we spend the rest of the afternoon on rides, including the Quack Attack, which is everything I knew it would be.

Our final stop is the Quackie Drop—a pool you can drop into from swing ropes, diving platforms set at various heights, and even a few inflatable duck-shaped trampolines.

Sig takes my hand. "Let's sit this one out."

Reaper goes to supervise the kids, along with a few employees.

Sig leads me toward a grouping of giant rubber duckies facing the pool. He settles astride a yellow duckie that's got a lion's mane and an extra-large bill, while I sit down next to him astride a purple alien duckie. It's a lot more fun than sitting on a bench—and it keeps me at a safe distance from the temptation of the man next to me.

I never thought I'd be into yellow board shorts, but they're hands down the hottest thing I've ever seen on a man. My gaze keeps drifting down to his six-pack abs and the tempting trail that dips into his waistband.

I lick my lips before I realize what I'm doing, and quickly look away.

We watch the kids in silence for some time. They cannonball into the pool, splash around, and act nothing like they had in the back yard this morning.

I owe it all to Sig.

"Thank you," I tell him softly.

"For what?" He sounds genuinely surprised.

"For this. For helping with the kids. For bringing us here."

"I think I needed this just as much as you all did," he says, surprising me. "I've worked so hard to build this place. I've taken jobs at dozens of water parks, went to business school, got investors..." He shakes his head. "I've been heading toward this moment all my life, but until today, it hasn't felt real." He shrugs. "It still doesn't feel real."

I tighten my thighs around the purple duckie, hold on to its ear for purchase, and lean toward him.

"What are you doing?" he asks, then lets out a yelp when I pinch his biceps. His deliciously muscular, warm, tempting biceps.

"It's real."

"I'm not sure if I should thank you or pinch you back."

"Definitely thank me," I say, prepared to jump off my duckie and run.

He smiles. "Thank you."

I can't help feeling a little disappointed.

The fact that I'd rather start a pinch war with the man next to me than have a grown-up conversation just emphasizes how unfit I am to be a guardian for Janey's kids.

I touch Janey's ring with a resigned sigh. "I make a terrible adult."

Chapter 6

Rachel

Sig gives me a sensual once-over. "I think you make a really great adult."

I snort and try to ignore the way my body heats in response. "Not what I meant."

"Okay, then humor me."

I gesture at the kids, who are laughing as they splash around in the pool. "I bet if I tried to join them, they'd start crying again."

"You were getting along great on the rides."

"They were having fun despite me, not because of me." I shake my head and my shoulders droop. "I've really let them down."

"Why would you say that?"

"I'm not sure where to start..."

"The beginning?"

I shrug and trace the wave shape of Janey's ring. "I'm not sure how much Ada told you, but her daughter, Janey—the kids' mom—was my best friend."

Sig nods.

It still hurts, thinking about her—talking about her—but the words spill out. "She got pregnant in our final year of college. She wanted five kids, at least, but then the car accident..." I swallow hard.

Sig leans toward me, but any thoughts of a pinch war are long forgotten. He takes my hand in his and gives it a squeeze. "I'm so sorry, Rachel."

"Thanks," I smile softly. "I was the kids' godmother. Chris—their dad—grew up in foster care. He didn't want that to ever happen to his kids, so they drafted a will. I promised to be their guardian, but it was just supposed to be for peace of mind not..." I tighten my grip on Sig's hand. "I never thought anything would happen to them. I'd only been out of college for a few years. I'd just finished my latest cruising contract and started on a backpacking trip through Europe when I got the news." I swallow hard. "I flew back for the funeral, but... I didn't stay."

Sig gives my hand another squeeze and lets me talk.

"If Ada wasn't in the picture, I would have stuck around. I swear I would have. I'd never have let anything happen to the kids."

"I know you wouldn't have," Sig readily agrees.

"But I was still so young, and Ada said the kids were all she had left, and she wanted them and I... I... got on that plane. The backpacking trip was a distraction. And then I went back to cruising and got paid to travel and work on my tan."

"Don't forget about all the hard work."

I glance at him in surprise. "Most people don't think of it as hard work."

"You're talking to a guy who's opening a water park. I've interviewed quite a few people who work on cruises."

I perk up. "Really?"

He nods. "Where did you work on the ship?"

"Mostly lessons at the pool."

Sig's eyes brighten considerably. "Swimming lessons?"

I laugh. "No. Scuba diving. On adult-only cruises. Which probably explains why I'm so bad with kids."

"I think you're great with kids," Sig lies. He has to be lying, because the last few days have proven I'm a train wreck.

My shoulders slump. "I'm really trying. I've been studying IT at night for the past year, and I finally got my certification last month."

"You have?" He sounds more confused than impressed.

"I've got a few interviews lined up," I add.

"You don't sound very excited about it."

"Honestly? I'm not." I try to picture myself trapped in front of a computer screen in some dimly lit basement. No sun. No water. No fun. "I'm doing it for the kids."

"You don't need to have a desk job to be there for the kids," Sig says.

"You don't get it, Sig. You own a water park! I don't even have a savings account. I've been spending everything I earn. Life is short. You never know how much time you've got. What kind of guardian does that make me?"

"Kids don't care about savings."

I slide off the duck. "But nanas do."

"Not the one I know. She's got a house and savings. The kids don't need money. They need you."

I shake my head and look away. They are in excellent hands with her. Just not with me.

"I think what you really need"—Sig slides off his duckie and pulls me into his arms—"is a distraction."

And then he covers my lips with his.

He catches me completely off guard as he claims my mouth in a fiery kiss, and just like before, I melt.

I forget where we are. I forget that I wasn't going to do this. I forget that I'm a responsible adult.

All I can think about is the feel of Sig's lips against mine. His hands running up and down my back.

Desire shoots through me.

I *want* him.

I *need* him.

I *can't*.

I pull away and instantly regret it.

No man has ever made me feel the way Sig does. I'm pretty sure no other man ever will.

But I still can't let this happen, I remind myself. *Not now. Maybe not ever.*

Sig stares down at me, his breath coming out in pants. His pupils are dilated, his gaze glued to my lips, and I almost kiss him again.

Almost.

"Sig…" I whisper softly and place my palms flat on his chest. "If I'd met you at any other time in my life, I would do this in a heartbeat. But I'm supposed to prove to Ada that I'm a responsible adult. I can't just hook up with the first hot guy I meet."

I don't think Sig really gets the point because he breaks into a slow grin. "You think I'm hot?"

I roll my eyes. Like the man hasn't looked in a mirror.

His grin widens. "And you want to hook up with me?"

My cheeks flush. "Of course I want to, but—"

"If hooking up is on the table"—Sig gives me a once-over so hot I almost self-combust—"or in a hot tub..." He gives me a slow, sexy wink. "I'm in."

I swallow hard, because I don't want to say no. I *really* don't. But I also don't have a choice. "I don't think you get what I'm trying to say."

"I think I do." He takes my hands in his. "Can I be upfront with you?"

I worry my lower lip and nod.

"I've wanted you from the moment I saw you. Naked, fully clothed, any way you'll have me."

My pulse spikes, but I shake my head. "I can't."

"Why?"

"I need to prove that I'm a responsible adult."

"It sounds more like you're trying to prove you're a *boring* adult when you're perfect just the way you are."

My shoulders slump. "You don't understand."

"I don't, but it's clearly important to you." He takes a step back with a sad smile. "Whatever you need, Rachel."

My heart sinks, even though this is exactly what I wanted. "I should join the kids. Assuming they want me around."

"Of course they do." Sig leads the way. When we reach the pool where the kids are throwing rubber ducks at each other, he claps his hands. "You three, out of the water and over here, now!"

To my surprise, they splash over without argument. And with huge grins on their faces, too.

Sig crosses his arms over his chest. "Okay, ducklings. Spill. Why are you giving Rachel a hard time?"

And just like that, they're back to frowning.

"Sig, don't," I hiss. "It's fine."

All I want is for the kids to be happy. And I'm willing to do whatever it takes to earn a place in their lives.

Sig frowns. "Don't you want to know what's going on?"

What's going on is that they hate me. They're glaring at me like they think I'm a monster. If I admit I don't know what I'm doing as a guardian, maybe they'll give me a break. At the very least, I can figure out what I did wrong so I can do better. For Janey.

I touch her ring for courage and turn to the kids. "What happened, you guys? We were having so much fun when I first got here. What changed?"

Lisa crosses her arms in front of her chest. "You know what changed, *Rachel*."

"Yeah, *Rachel*," Noah says, copying her.

I glance at Sig, then back at the kids. I have no clue what they're talking about, and he comes to my rescue.

"If you want to come back to Rubber Duckie World, you're going to explain."

I wait for them to tell him I'm a terrible godmother and I don't know how to act around kids and that every word out of my mouth is wrong and they wish I'd just leave.

But then Anna clears her throat. Her voice shakes as she says, "We just want Nana back."

My heart squeezes painfully in my chest. "She'll be back before you know it."

"No, she won't," Noah cries. "You're lying!"

Lisa glares at me. "You made Nana leave, and you're going to make sure she never comes back."

"I would never do that!"

Noah stomps his foot and clenches his little hands into fists. "We heard you on the phone!"

Anna nods emphatically. "When she called on Monday, we heard everything."

I shake my head as I wrack my brain to try to recall what I might have said. Finally I settle on, "I don't know what you think you heard, but Nana is coming back."

"You're lying!" Lisa shouts. "You want to take us away from our nana, and we won't let you!"

Noah whimpers.

Anna starts to cry.

And I turn pleading eyes on Sig, because now I'm completely out of my element, and I have no clue what to do.

Chapter 7

Sig

Rachel's lower lip trembles, and I have the sudden urge to kiss away her tears. *Focus, Duck!*

Anna and Noah are openly bawling. Lisa looks like she's about to break down, too. And as for poor Reaper? The man keeps glancing longingly at Quackie Drop. I really wouldn't blame him if he decided to jump. Hell, if this wasn't my ducking problem, I would, too.

"You have to believe me," Rachel pleads, her beautiful face stained with tears. "I would never try to take you kids away from your nana. I can't do this on my own!"

"You're lying!" Lisa shouts.

Fuck a duckity duck.

This is all my fault. Why couldn't I leave well enough alone? The kids were happy. They were freshly showered. They were giving Rachel minimal trouble. Things were going well... and the four of them could have gone home with some happy quacking memories and rubber duckie memorabilia.

But I just had to butt in...

I take in the tear-fest, completely at a loss. Rachel would never force the kids to leave their nana. And she wouldn't lie to me about it. I'm sure of it.

Rachel is the person I'm meant to be with. My other half. The love of my life. My fated mate.

I'm already falling for her, and have been from the moment our eyes met and I knew she was mine.

I've dreamed of finding my mate since I first shifted. And the magic weaving between us tells me she's a good, kind person, who's perfect for me. Which means that whatever's going on must be a big misunderstanding.

I step closer to the woman I plan to spend the rest of my life with and try to physically reassure since I can't do it with words. It might alienate the kids, and I need to fix things. "Kids, I think I'm going to need you to explain. What, exactly, did you hear Rachel say that makes you think she's trying to take you away from Nana?"

"We don't think she's *trying*. We know she *is*," Lisa snaps.

Anna sniffles, nods, and says something so softly I don't catch it. I lean closer, and she says it again. "She said she wants custody."

"Custody?" I repeat with a confused glance at Rachel.

She looks taken aback, and I'm honestly not sure what to think.

Lisa scowls at her. "She sent Nana on the cruise so she could get custody while she's away."

Rachel's eyes widen and her fingers fly to her ring, tracing its wavelike shape. "I would never do that."

"Nana told us you paid for her cruise ticket," Lisa accuses. "And we know she didn't want to go at first, but you convinced her to go."

Rachel nods. "Yes, but not so I could take you away. I would never, ever want to do that. I just thought Ada could use a few weeks to relax. And I wanted to take care of you kids to prove to her that I'm a responsible adult."

Responsible adult. There are those words again. The ones Rachel equates with giving up her own happiness and locking herself up in some office and working a job I know she'd hate.

"I just wanted to show Ada I'm ready to stay, so I could help her raise you kids. But I was wrong," she adds, her lower lip trembling. "What was I thinking? I'll never be responsible. I couldn't even get you to shower without Sig's help."

I hate to see her so sad, so I say the first thing that comes to mind. "Baths are better."

Not even a smile.

Rachel drops to her knees in front of the kids. "I would never, *ever* want to take you guys away from Nana. I just want to stay, too. I'm done traveling. I'm done packing up and leaving after each visit. I want to be your guardian. *With* Nana, not instead of her. Please say you'll give me another shot."

Her voice quavers, and ducking tears spring to my eyes. Duck stereotypes. Grown men cry. Especially during emotional moments with their fated mate and her kids.

But Lisa shakes her head. "If you really wanted to move in with us, you wouldn't need custody."

Rachel shakes her head. "Your parents left you in my care, Lisa. I gave up custody when I left. But I want it back so I can always be here for you. *With* Nana. Not instead of her. Never instead of her!"

Rachel's voice breaks, and I place a comforting hand on her shoulder, lending my silent support. Her skin is warm beneath my palm, and I have to fight the urge to pull her into my arms and hold her tight until she feels better.

She shoots me a half-smile, and that's enough.

She turns back to the kids. "Please tell me you'll give me a chance?"

The kids exchange looks, as if they're not sure what to think, and Rachel's shoulders droop.

I shoot Reaper a look that screams help, because I'm fresh out of ideas, and he glances at the pool. Is he telling me he wishes he could swim away? Or is he telling me that the best thing for everyone is a nice refreshing swim?

He's definitely not telling me to cannonball into the pool and duck in mid-air. Though if I did, that would distract everyone. And lighten the mood. Or seriously freak out Rachel, considering she didn't take it well last time. But a repeat performance might do the trick. And if I plan to make her and the kids my family, they'll need to know about my duck side eventually. So why not right here, right now?

I get ready to shift, but Anna beats me to it. Not by shifting, since she's definitely human. She's also far too young to have a shifted form even if she were a Bayan like me.

She speaks up, voice trembling, "So Nana really is coming back?"

"Of course!" Rachel nods emphatically. "When she calls tonight, she'll tell you so herself."

The kids exchange hopeful glances, and some of the tension seems to seep out of Rachel.

I forget all about shifting and let this moment be about them, not me.

Noah wipes his tear-stained cheeks with the back of his hand. "Does that mean you'll stay in our house?" he asks Rachel.

She nods.

"Well, you can't stay in my room." He pouts, and it's hard to keep a straight face. The kid is adorable!

Lisa rolls her eyes. "Rachel wouldn't take our rooms, *Noah*," she tells her little brother.

I don't miss the fact that a few minutes earlier, she was emphasizing Rachel's name the same way. Girl's got attitude, but she's a good kid.

She turns to Rachel, "Where will you stay?"

Rachel chuckles. "I'm fine on the couch for now. I'm planning to find an rental nearby."

"You don't have to do that. You can stay at my place," I blurt.

Her surprised deer-in-headlights expression tells me I'm coming on too strong.

"I have a spare room," I quickly add, even though that's not what I want. I want this woman in my bed. In my house. In my life. In my future.

I want us to break down the walls between our two houses and combine them so there's enough space for all of us, Nana and all the babies we'll have included. Or we could always buy a bigger house. After we get married.

But Rachel's human. I can't expect her to instantly be on board with our relationship like a shifter would be. She doesn't have the built-in faith that the magic would never steer us astray. I have to give her time to catch up.

And judging by the panic in Rachel's eyes, she's going to need a lot of it. But I'm up to the challenge, and I plan to romance her and make her mine.

For now, I shrug, like it's no big deal. "Think about it," I tell her.

Then I back off while she talks with the kids. After a lot more questions and hugs all around, I kneel in front of the kids. "Okay, you three. I want your word that you won't give Rachel any more trouble. And that means daily baths."

"Or showers," Rachel quickly jumps in.

"Baths," I repeat, using my no-nonsense voice.

Noah grins. "Showers are for chumps. Right, Sig?"

"Right. And I want you in school every day, no arguments, you hear me?"

They nod emphatically.

Rachel and I share a smile, and I get to my feet. "Now, who wants to stop by the gift shop before we head home? I think there are some rubber duckies with your names on them. One each. On the house."

The kids cheer, and the moment I point them in the right direction, they take off. A very relieved-looking Reaper follows. The man can manage a fully staffed kitchen, but give him an upset child, and he falls apart.

Rachel and I follow, and she grins up at me. There's a pep in her step that wasn't there earlier. It's like a weight has been lifted off her shoulders and the sun has come out from behind the clouds. Which just goes to show how exhausting fighting with the kids must have been for her.

Rachel's eyes twinkle, and that spark makes her a hundred times more gorgeous and irresistible. It takes everything in me not to pull her into my arms and claim her right on the spot.

She threads her fingers through mine, and my self-control almost snaps. "Thank you, Sig," she says softly. "Seriously. You don't know how stressed I've been."

"I can imagine." Because the difference really is like night and day.

I can also see this woman working on a cruise and traveling the world. And I don't want her to lose that joy. Not when she doesn't have to.

I pull her to a stop and turn to face her. "Rachel, I want you to be happy."

"I *am* happy, thanks to you!" She smiles broadly up at me.

"I don't mean right now. I mean always." I take her other hand in mine. "Being a responsible adult doesn't mean you have to give up your own happiness. Responsible doesn't have to mean boring. You can still travel. Have fun. Work by the pool. Those things won't make you a bad guardian. And an office job won't make you a good one."

"I know..." She sighs. "But I need a steady income. And I don't want to cruise anymore, not if it takes me away from the kids."

"Then come work at Rubber Duckie World."

It's the perfect solution. I own the most fun place in the world. But Rachel shakes her head. "You don't have to give me a job, Sig."

"I don't have to. I want to. And you'd be good at it." At her skeptical look, I add, "You have experience."

"Giving scuba lessons to adults isn't experience."

"Transferable skills, then. And you can learn to run the rides or give tours. There are so many different jobs at a waterpark, and they're all better than a desk job." The thought of being cooped up in an office all day makes my heart hurt.

Rachel hesitates, and for a second I think I've gotten through to her, but then she shakes her head. "Sig, I appreciate it. I really do. But I need to figure this out on my own. And I've spent a year studying IT. I'm actually kind of good at it. I don't know if I'll like it. Maybe I won't. But I at least want to give it a shot."

"Then I'm with you." And I am. I'll always support her, no matter what. It's just too soon to tell her. But it doesn't stop me from blurting out, "Would you give me a shot, too? Just to get to know you better. *Please?*"

I sound like a desperate fool and feel a sudden urge to jump into the Quackie River, shift, and let the current take me away. But I'm glad that I don't, because Rachel breaks into a huge grin.

Her next words floor me. "I'd like that, too."

Chapter 8

Rachel

The next morning, Sig comes over bright and early and keeps me from burning the eggs and setting the toast on fire. Breakfast is a blast. The kids no longer hate me, and everything goes as smoothly as the butter we spread on Sig's perfectly golden slices of toast.

I'm convinced the man can do anything until I find out he can't drive. His cheeks flush an adorable pink as he admits he doesn't have his license. And he still seems a little flustered as I maneuver Ada's old van out of the driveway and drop the kids off at school.

The old clunker doesn't have Bluetooth, so Sig takes charge of the radio. And since the A/C doesn't work, we roll down our windows to keep cool. Both are a pain, and I add a vehicle upgrade to the top of my mental list of things I plan to save up for once I find work.

I can't blame the van for how torturous the drive is. That's all Sig's fault.

My traitorous hands long to touch the man sitting next to me, and I hold on to the steering wheel like a lifeline, so I don't do something I regret. But how am I supposed to resist his just-rolled-out-of-bed hair or those tanned, muscular biceps? It's like he's begging to be touched. I long to squeeze his muscular thigh and run my hand up... up... up... until...

I gulp and grip the steering wheel so hard my knuckles turn white.

As the week goes on, driving with a temptation of a man like Sig gets increasingly more difficult. And the kisses definitely don't help. We sneak them in every chance we get—before the kids are up, after they go to bed, and everywhere in between—each one more toe-curling than the last.

The urge to forget about being a responsible adult and hook up with the man grows. But I constantly remind myself that the kids come first. I need to focus all my energy on getting my life together... and job applications aren't going to send themselves.

Sig convinces me to work on my resume at Rubber Duckie World, on a pool-side duckie desk. It's surprisingly comfortable, and the giant, bright-yellow parasol provides some much-needed shade, so my laptop doesn't overheat.

I spend each morning looking for jobs while trying not to ogle Sig. He's completely in his element, whether he's training staff, directing the crew filming promotional material, or setting up for Sunday's rubber duckie race.

At lunch time, we hit a few of the rides, starting with my all-time favorite: Quack Attack. Then we head over to Duckie Diner to sample Reaper's mouthwatering, duck-themed creations. The guy's a genius in the kitchen and a genuinely great guy, so it comes to me as no surprise that he and Sig have been lifelong friends.

Over lunch, I learn that they grew apart when Reaper got married to a horrible-sounding woman, and then reconnected after the divorce. I also find out that Reaper's real name is Rupert—though I'm sworn to secrecy under threat of a lifetime Duckie Diner ban—and I also learn what Sig is short for.

"Sigvart," I repeat when he tells me. "I like that."

He grins. "It's actually my middle name, after Grandad."

"The duckie collector?"

Sig nods. "I idolized him as a kid—still do. And William doesn't suit me."

I'm inclined to agree.

We talk a bit more about Sig's grandad and his childhood in a small town compared to mine in the big city. I tell him about college, and when he asks about my ring, I explain that Ada got it as a high school graduation present for Janey, and that she left it for me in her will along with her kids. Then we lighten the mood and compare our past jobs—mine aboard cruise ships, and Sig's at various amusement parks.

By Wednesday morning, we've settled into a routine, which gets broken up when the principal pulls me aside. But instead of more lectures and veiled threats, she admits she was wrong.

"She said she misjudged me. And she thinks I'm doing a great job with the kids," I gush as I settle behind the wheel. "And she's glad they've got me. Can you believe it?"

"Of course I can." Sig places a hand over mine. "You are doing a great job with them, Rachel. And they're lucky to have you. We all are!"

I'm still thinking about his words when we pick up the kids after school, cook dinner—all Sig, since I can't follow a recipe to save my life—and grab water guns so we can chase each other around the back yard, shouting and laughing until the sun sets.

On Thursday night—after another perfect day with Sig and the kids—it rains, so we decide to have a living room dance party, complete with a half-pineapple, half-sane pizza. And when the kids start fighting over music, Sig intervenes, mediates, and keeps the peace. He helps with bedtime, and once the kids are asleep, we slow dance the night away.

I almost ask him to spend the night. Almost. But it's a terrible idea, so I fall asleep on the couch alone, dreaming of being pressed up against Sig's hard chest, his powerful arms wrapped around me and his hot lips on mine.

Friday morning brings sunshine, clear skies, and drenched panties. I take care of myself in the shower, try not to blush while Sig and I make breakfast, and go upstairs to wake up the kids. I keep my hands to myself during school drop-off, but the moment we get to Rubber Duckie World, he pulls me into his arms and kisses me like he's drowning and I'm air.

When we pull apart, I'm breathless and every one of my reservations melts away.

"I have something to show you." Sig takes my hand and guides me toward a quiet area of the park. We stop in front of a locked gate, and he punches in the security code. 382543. "Welcome to my personal section of the park. I built it for whenever I need to get away and be alone. No one else is allowed through here."

I peer past the fence, but from my vantage point, all I see is a winding path. "Do you want to be alone?"

"Yes," he says, and my heart sinks. "With you."

I can't help but smile as he leads me inside. "So what's through here?"

"Lazy river, a pool, and a giant personal bathtub. With a hundred and fifty custom rubber duckies."

His eyes light up when he mentions his collection, but my mind is as far away from duckies as it can get. "You have a giant bathtub?"

"Filled with bubbles and duckies."

"One hundred and fifty duckies," I can't help but tease.

"Only fifty are in the tub. There are seventy-five in the lazy river and ten in the pool. The other fifteen are extra-large duckies for lounging. There are four by the pool, four by the hot tub, and seven along the river."

The fact that the man has an exact duckie count is kind of endearing. "I wish I had something I was as passionate about as you are about duckies."

Sig pauses mid-step. "You don't?"

I shake my head. "I would have mentioned it if I had."

We resume walking in silence. Sig leads me toward the pool, tosses his shirt on the hot concrete and kicks off his flip-flops. My eyes are glued to his abs and the trail of hair leading into his swim trunks when he adds, "There has to be something."

"Huh?"

"Your duckie thing."

"I really don't have one."

He frowns and dives into the crystal-clear water, but by the time he rests his forearms on the edge, he's grinning. "Come on in. The water's perfect."

I pull my sundress over my head to reveal my pink bikini, unbuckle the cute sandals I got on a day trip in Costa Rica, and dive in.

The water is cold and refreshing. I get used to it by the time I surface and float up to Sig, feeling relaxed and happy.

"You must have a duckie thing," he says. "*Everyone* does." When I frown, he adds, "Not necessarily a collection like mine. Just that one thing that means more to you than anything else."

I think of the kids. Of the man in the water next to me. Of Ada. "Family."

"Family doesn't count," Sig says instantly. Like he doesn't even have to think about it. Like no one will ever matter to him as much as his duckies.

"Of course, family counts!"

"I didn't mean it like that. Family always comes first."

"I hear a but in there somewhere..."

"There isn't." He runs a hand through his hair, which is more brown than blond now that it's wet.

Despite my annoyance with him, I'm drawn to the man like a kid to a water slide. I long to run my fingers through his drenched locks, trace them along his chiseled jawline, and pull him in for a kiss.

"Rachel..." The way he says my name, his voice filled with emotion, makes my heart race. "I'd give this place up in a heartbeat for the people I love."

My heart skips a beat and then starts racing double-time.

He doesn't mean me, I remind myself. *He doesn't love me.*

We've barely known each other for a week. It's too soon. We're just two neighbors who are getting to know each other, with make-out sessions in between. We haven't even had sex.

And yet every part of me wants this man to say that I matter more to him than the duckies surrounding us.

He lets go of the pool's edge and treads water. "What if you had to pick one thing that you love most, but you couldn't pick people?"

I tread water too. "You're really not going to drop this one, are you?"

Sig smiles sheepishly. "It's important."

"Okay. Fine. Cruise ships."

"Full size or collectibles?"

"The kind that can take me places..." I say, and instantly feel guilty because cruising is the reason why I wasn't there for the kids all these years. I grab the edge of the pool again. "Look, Sig. I get that collecting duckies is important to you, but I don't plan on collecting cruise ships or anything else." I plan on getting a steady job and taking care of Noah, Anna, and Lisa.

"That's what I'm worried about." Sig slides below the water's surface and then resurfaces with a splash.

I frown. "Worried? Why?"

He purses his lips.

In the week that I've known him, there's been a palpable connection between us. Each moment, each conversation... everything between us has felt right... until now.

Sig seems to realize it, too, because his expression turns serious. "Rachel, we need to talk."

A heavy feeling settles in my gut. Everyone knows there's only one reason a man would ever say 'we need to talk.' Sig is breaking up with me!

Not that we're actually together. We were just getting to know each other.

My heart doesn't seem to care.

It doesn't make sense. Why does Sig care that I don't collect duckies or cruise ships or whatnot?

Maybe it's not about collecting things. Maybe he's finally realized that he's got his life together, and I don't. He owns an entire water park, and I don't even have a job. But he's the one who made me realize that I don't need those things. And now he's dumping me over it? *Seriously?*

At least it's happening now, after a week, before I got really invested in us. *But then why does it hurt so much?*

I'm no stranger to being dumped. One time, the guy I'd been seeing did it in bed, while we were both still naked. Sig and I haven't even had sex. I shouldn't care!

So then why does this feel different? Why does being with Sig feel different?

Don't cry, Rachel. You barely know each other!

But in my heart, it feels like we've known each other forever... Like we're two parts of a whole who fit together to become one.

I want to be one with Sig. I want him naked. I want him in my life. I want him forever.

My eyes widen as the realization slams into me like a wave. Somehow, in the span of a week, without even sleeping together, I've managed to fall in love with Sig.

And I'm about to get my heart shattered into a million pieces...

Chapter 9

Sig

Rachel grabs the edge of the pool and pulls herself up like a goddess. Water streams down her delicious body, and my eyes snap to her hot, round ass.

She looks so ducking hot in that pink bikini. The way it clings to her body when she turns around makes me rock hard, and I'm glad I'm submerged in the pool so she can't see the tent in my trunks.

"You don't have to say anything, Sig," she says breezily. "We've only known each other a week. If you're not interested in pursuing whatever this thing is between us—"

"I *am* interested," I snap. A bit too loudly.

She frowns. Like she's the one who actually doesn't want this.

"We're good together, Rachel." *More than you know.* "I want this. I want us."

I'm about to climb out of the pool... Wrap her in my arms... Beg if I have to... when she sits down on the edge next to me and dips her long legs in the water. "What was up with that whole conversation, Sig? Why do we need to talk?"

I grimace.

How do I explain that I'm a shifter who transforms into a rubber duckie? And that if I take her home, the magic will turn her into a shifter, too? Not a duckie shifter, like me. No, she'll be something else. Possibly a ducking cruise ship, and a full-sized one, minus the ducking part.

I rub my temples, because it hurts my head just thinking about it.

How the duck am I going to explain it all to Rachel? I shouldn't, that's how. I should give this thing between us a couple of months. Make sure we're solid.

But she looks so frustrated with me, all because of the things I've kept from her. And I'm tired of lying. Terrified I'll accidentally shift in front of her again and make it all so much worse than it needs to be.

"Follow me." I climb out of the pool. Last thing I need is for Rachel to freak out, fall in, and drown while I'm duckied out and unable to shift.

She may be an amazing swimmer, but based on how she reacted the first time she saw me shift, I wouldn't put it past her.

Once we're safely away from any bodies of water, I turn to face her, knowing this is my last chance to change my mind.

The past few days have been amazing. Perfect. They could be that way for a long, long time. All

I have to do is stay in my human form. Date her. Enjoy our time together. Pretend to be someone I'm not.

It feels wrong. So wrong...

I need her and the kids to know the real me. That way I'm not constantly tense, waiting for something to startle me and force me to shift, worried that I'll freak them out and lose them forever.

Quit going in circles and duck the duck up!

That's it. I'm doing this!

I take a deep breath. And shift.

Rachel shrieks.

I shift back.

She shrieks again.

I shift once more.

This time, she doesn't scream.

She rubs her eyes, like she thinks she's imagining things.

I shift a few more times, to make it clear this is real.

Eyes wide, voice hopeful, she whispers, "Whoa, those are some crazy special effects. Couldn't you have given me some warning?"

"Not special effects," I tell her, and shift once more.

When I shift back, she shakes her head. "There was an amazing magician aboard the ship last year, but she's got nothing on you."

I pull Rachel into my arms, press my lips against hers, and wonder how kissing her can feel so magical every time. Then, I shift.

My arms disappear from around her, and I duck at her feet. If that's not going to convince her, I don't know what is.

She kneels in front of me and pokes my side. "How'd you do that?" She looks around. "Where'd you go?"

Since I can't talk in rubber duckie form, I shift back—and find her kneeling with her sweet little mouth in front of my crotch.

Fuck a double duck! A very hard double duck, because the duckie in my swim trunks springs to attention the moment he thinks he might get some mouth action.

Rachel's eyes widen as she takes in my hard-on. She licks her lips.

I pull her to her feet before she decides to yank down my swim trunks and pretend rubber duckie shifters aren't real.

Her cheeks flush. "How'd you pull off that trick?"

"You mean get a hard-on?"

She giggles. "I meant the magic trick!"

"It's not a trick. It's *actual* magic. I'm a rubber duckie shifter."

"A rubber duckie shifter..." she repeats softly.

I demonstrate.

Bam, duckie. Bam, human. Bam duckie. Bam human.

"I shift into a rubber duckie," I say, even though it's pretty obvious.

"You shift into a rubber duckie..." she repeats.

I wonder if I've broken her.

Several moments pass in silence. A rock forms in the pit of my stomach, because I've misjudged things. I thought this was the right thing to do, but any minute now, she'll run away screaming, and I'll never see her again. Never get to talk to her, or touch her, or be with her.

I pull her into my arms, possibly for the last time, and hold my breath, terrified to let go.

"So..." she says against my chest. "You're like... a kid-friendly version of a werewolf?"

"Not that kid friendly." I pull back and give her a once-over. And the boulder in my gut breaks apart and floats away on the backs of a hundred rubber duckies. "But I guess you could say that."

"How's that even possible?"

"I grew up in Shifter Bay." For a supernatural, it would be explanation enough. Since Rachel's human, I add, "Everyone from Shifter Bay shifts into the one thing they love most."

"And you love rubber duckies." It's not a question. It doesn't need to be. My love for duckies is everywhere.

"Hell yeah!" And you might shift into a full-sized cruise ship... something I can't quite wrap my head around.

Rachel bites her lower lip as she mulls my duckie news over. "Does Reaper know?"

I nod. "He shifts into a hot pepper."

Rachel bursts out laughing, and the sound fills my heart with joy. "Wait, are you serious?"

I nod.

"Okay."

"Okay?" I repeat.

"Okay, you shift into a rubber duckie, and Reaper shifts into a hot pepper." She shoots me one of her adorable smiles.

"Are you sure you're okay with it? Last time you saw me shift you..."

"Freaked out? I mean, can you blame me? I thought the kids had literally driven me insane. I was sure I hallucinated the whole thing. I thought I was having a mental breakdown!"

I pull her into my arms. "You're not crazy, baby."

She snuggles against my chest. "Well, now I know that..."

"There's one more thing," I whisper into her hair. Not the cruise ship part—that's a problem for another time. "You're my fated mate."

"Fated mate..." Rachel breathes.

These days, practically everyone's read or watched something to do with fated mates. Usually, a romance with animal shifters or the occasional vampire. So Rachel should know exactly what I mean.

Then again, Reaper once found a series of Aussie novellas where fated mates were couples who broke up because they were meant to be 'just mates,' the Australian word for 'friends'... and no way am I risking Rachel mistaking what I'm saying for that clusterduck.

"We're supernatural soulmates, Rachel. We're meant to be." I take her hand and place it over my heart. "I can feel it right here."

Rachel stares up at me, her lips forming a sexy 'O', her eyes wide. "We're really fated mates?" she repeats. "Like in books?"

"Depends which ones you read."

Her cheeks flush an adorable pink, and she licks her lips as her gaze drops to my tented swim trunks.

I give her a slow grin. "I'm going to need to read whatever you've been reading."

Her blush deepens. Called it.

She shakes her head, and her eyes get a faraway look. "Fated mates..."

It's kind of adorable, how she repeats things to process them. I like knowing that about her, and I can't wait to learn all the little things that are uniquely Rachel.

"I know you might not believe me yet," I tell her. "But I plan to spend every day proving to you that we're perfect together. I'll wait for as long as it takes for you to accept it."

I'll wait forever for you, Rachel.

Rachel stares up at me, and I get lost in her hazel eyes. "I already know we're perfect together."

This time, it's my turn to be surprised. "You do?"

She nods. "I felt it the moment our eyes met."

I gape at her. "You felt the mate bond?"

"Kind of..." Her cheeks flush. "I was drawn to you. Physically, at first. But as I got to know you..." Her blush intensifies, and I realize she's not ready to admit her feelings for me.

So I cup the back of her head, loving the feel of her wet hair against my palm, and kiss her.

My first thought is that I could drown in Rachel's lips, and this is coming from a man who can't drown. No joke.

I plan to take advantage of that particular talent by using my tongue on my mate while she's in the tub.

Or in one of the VIP pools. Or on an inflatable duck in the lazy river, if that's where she'll have me.

Because I'll take Rachel however I can get her. I just have to get her naked first.

We kiss until we're both breathless and panting. I'm so hard it hurts, and my hand has somehow found its way beneath her bikini top. Her sweet moans echo around us, and I want to take her on the spot and duck her till she comes.

Now that everything's out in the open, the urge to claim her is overwhelming. She's my fated mate. I've accepted her, and she's accepted me. All of me. But fucking her on the scalding hot sidewalk is a painfully bad idea. And I don't want to rush her and scare her away.

I should take her on a proper date first, complete with candles, Champagne, and music. But it'll have to wait because I want her too much to stop.

The duckie in my pants begs me to set him free, and I plan to—as soon as I get my mate good and ready. And I know just the place.

I force myself to pull away. She starts to protest, but I silence her with another kiss and whisper an invitation against her lips. "Join me for a bubble bath?"

The smile she gives me is breathtaking. "I'd love to."

And I love you. I just don't say it out loud. Not yet.

Chapter 10

Rachel

Sig threads his fingers through mine and leads me toward the hot tub. It's shaped like a giant bathtub and filled with bubbles and dozens of rubber duckies.

My heart thunders loudly as I stare at the tub. "Seventy-five duckies, right?"

"Fifty, actually. Seventy-five is the lazy river."

"Right," I say. My voice quavers.

"If you don't want to do this—"

"I do. I want to." I grab Sig's strong shoulders and pull him closer. I tangle one hand through his wet hair, stand on my tiptoes, and press my lips hungrily against his.

I can't resist the electric chemistry between us, but I also can't quite wrap my mind around the fact that the man I want shifts into a rubber duckie.

If Sig hadn't transformed while his lips were on mine, I still wouldn't believe it. But I know I'm not going crazy. Sig is definitely real, supernatural, and the most skilled and intoxicating kisser I've ever met.

He cups the back of my neck and ravages my lips hungrily as his other hand traces tantalizingly slow circles around my nipple, massaging it through my bikini top.

I arch into his touch and moan in pleasure. Every nerve in my body is on fire, begging for more, but just when I think I can't take it anymore and I'm about to grab his hand and slide it right where I want it, he pulls away, leaving me aching with desire.

"Come on." He takes my hand and guides me into the steamy tub. The water envelops us in its warmth as he guides me to the edge of the tub.

The jets pulsate against my skin, sending shivers through me as he pulls me onto his lap. His hands roam over my body as I straddle him, the hot bulge in his swim trunks rubbing against my core. I feel every inch of his desire beneath me and pump my hips, rubbing myself against him as the pleasure builds.

"Not yet." Sig grabs my hips and keeps me still, then his lips hungrily meet mine.

"More," I moan. "Please."

Sig pulls me off his lap and settles me on the bench. Warm water jets massage my back as Sig slips underwater and disappears beneath a sea of bubbles and duckies.

"What are you—"

That's as far as I get before his hands are on me. He slides my bikini bottoms to the side and slips a finger inside me. I moan and clench around it, then let out a surprised cry when he runs his tongue along my slit.

"Sig!" I try to pull him back up. "The s-soap," I moan as he sucks on my clit. "Air."

I need him to come up for air!

But it's almost like the man doesn't need to breathe. Or maybe he's so good he can make ten seconds of pleasure feel like an eternity.

He teases my clit with the tip of his tongue and pumps his finger in and out of my pussy, over and over again.

Five. Six. Seven. Eight.

I count each time he fingers me—proof that more time has passed—but Sig doesn't resurface. He also doesn't stop.

The pleasure builds alongside my panic. I grab fistfuls of his hair, but before I can yank him up, he slips a second finger inside me.

"Oh yes. Just like that." My hips fly up off the bench, and I forget that I'm in a hot tub and Sig is still underwater, and he needs to come up for air.

All I can do is ride his fingers, seeking release. Twenty-five. Twenty-six. Twenty-seven.

He needs to breathe!

But if he was running out of air, he wouldn't be using his tongue on my clit.

"More," I plead, hoping he can hear me underwater. "I'm so close. Please, Sig. Please."

Desperate for release, I yank on his hair. Not to pull him out of the water, but to keep him right where I need him.

And boy does he deliver.

I whimper and grind against his face, begging his magical tongue to keep licking me, just like that, until the pleasure builds and explodes through me in a tidal wave.

I scream, the sound echoing through the water park. Luckily, Sig gave all the staff the day off in preparation for tomorrow, so there isn't anyone around to hear me aside from the fifty duckies watching me as they bob on the water's surface.

Luckily, none of them are shifters—or, at least, I hope they're not. And I'm honestly too spent to care.

I sag back against the side of the Jacuzzi. The massage jets hit my back, and I let out a satisfied sigh.

Sig resurfaces a split second later, an equally satisfied grin on his face. I expect him to suck in a huge breath, or at least wipe the soap bubbles from his eyes, but aside from the smug look, the man acts like he wasn't just underwater, giving me the most magical orgasm of my life.

"How long can you hold your breath?" I ask.

"Forever."

"No, seriously."

"I am being serious." He smiles sheepishly. "It's one of my shifter powers. I don't need to breathe when I'm underwater."

"One of your shifter powers? Does that mean you have others?"

"Just one. I'll show you." He lifts me up off the bench like I weigh nothing and gives me a slow, lazy kiss, which quickly turns heated.

"Tell me you want me, Rachel," he demands.

"I want you, Sig. So much."

He rubs his hard length against my core, and my eyes widen.

When did he have time to ditch his swim trunks?

His impressive cock peeks out from amidst a sea of bubbles and duckies, and I reach for it.

I cup his throbbing length and stroke up and down. He lets out a surprised gasp that sounds almost like a squeak. And the fact that I have this power over him is intoxicating.

"Enough." Sig grabs my wrist and pins my arm behind my back.

My eyes widen and a wave of desire courses through me as he settles me on his cock and claims me like a man possessed.

I dig my nails into his slick back as he thrusts, each movement more powerful than the last. The heat and steam from the hot tub only add to the intensity.

I gasp and arch my back, pushing my breasts into his chest when Sig suddenly pulls me off his erection and spins me around so my back is to him.

"Trust me," he growls in my ear, his voice low and full of promise.

I nod, because I do. Even though I haven't known Sig long, I trust him implicitly.

He pins my arms behind my back with one powerful hand and slides inside me. Then he grabs a rubber duckie from the hot tub's surface and presses it against my clit.

Before I can react, the plastic toy begins to vibrate. The sensation shoots through my body, sending shockwave after shockwave of pleasure coursing through me. I clench around his cock and scream my release, my body shaking and legs trembling so hard I'd sink into the water if Sig wasn't holding me up.

"You liked that, didn't you?" His hot breath caresses my ear.

All I can do is nod.

"Good." He lifts me up and spins me around to face him.

His eyes glint with a mixture of satisfaction and desire as he lifts me up and settles me on the tip of his cock.

He thrusts into me with a fierceness that takes my breath away. Harder, deeper, he pushes me closer and closer to the edge all over again.

The water sloshes around us, and I almost miss his whispered words.

"I love you, Rachel."

I clench around his hard length, his words sending me right over the edge. The orgasm ripples through me, my muscles clenching around him as he continues to thrust.

And then I can't hold back the words. "I love you too, Sig."

His cock swells inside me at my words, and he tightens his grip around me. With one final deep thrust, he comes with a bellow so loud it causes several birds to take flight.

I sag against him, completely spent, then gasp as I feel him swell inside me again.

"Did you just…"

Sig chuckles. "Remember that other shifter power I mentioned?"

I nod, eyes wide.

"Just like a rubber duckie, I always bounce back."

I giggle.

"Rubber duckies are no laughing matter." He slides out of me and slams back into me, hard.

"I wasn't laughing—"

He slams into me again.

"I know you weren't laughing," he says, pupils dilated, dark stormy eyes locked on mine. "Because I was about to make you scream."

And, true to his word, he does. Over and over again, with his cock, with his mouth, with his fingers. Until I'm so exhausted, I start to doze off. Only then does he settle me on his lap, his hard cock still inside me.

He gazes into my eyes. "I meant what I said earlier, Rachel."

My mind is too fuzzy to follow, so I just shake my head.

"I love you," he declares, looking at me with such intensity that I can't help but blush.

"I—"

"Let me finish," he interrupts, placing a finger over my lips. "I don't want you to say it back unless you really mean it, okay? Because I know you only said it—"

"Sig—"

"In the heat of the moment! But—"

"Sig—"

"Shh, let me finish. I meant every word of what I said."

"Sig!"

He stops and raises an eyebrow slightly.

"I love you."

His face lights up, but he still looks unsure. "You don't have to say it back right now. I'll give you time."

"I love you," I repeat. "I don't need time. I fell for you the moment I saw you, and I've been falling for you more and more with every moment."

He hugs me tight, and it feels like everything in my life finally falls into place. "Will you spend forever with me, Rachel?"

I nod. "Forever sounds perfect."

Epilogue

Nine Months Later

I lean back on the couch and smile at Sig, who's duckied out on the living room floor, surrounded by building blocks.

The night Ada returned from her cruise, he'd shifted in front of Noah and the twins for the first time. And received the sort of instant acceptance that only kids can give. Then he shifted in front of their nana, and let's just say, she took it much better than I did.

It's been almost nine months since that day, and we've visited Sig's home of Shifter Bay twice, but the kids still get excited every time he shifts. And, luckily for them, Sig loves spending time in rubber duckie form.

Noah scoops Duckie Sig up and moves him toward the castle he and his sisters have just built. "He doesn't fit."

Lisa scowls at the hole in one of the walls. "Told you the door's too small. Didn't I say so, Rachel?"

"You did," I agree as I idly tap my fingers on the parenting book that I'm decidedly *not* reading. It's hard to focus with three kids around, a baby kicking my ribs, and a book drier than a slice of burned toast—which I haven't had the misfortune of eating since Sig took over breakfast.

I smile.

Because book or no book, I'm going to be a good guardian... and a good mom to the little boy we've got on the way. I believe it more and more with each passing day, and I know that with Sig by my side, I can't fail. He's a supportive husband, an amazing guardian, and I know he's going to be a wonderful dad. To all our kids, once the adoption goes through.

Plus, it doesn't hurt that he knows exactly what he's doing in the bedroom... and in the hot tub.

Even nine months after meeting him, I marvel at the fact that this is my life. I've gone from struggling at adulting, to marrying a man who surpasses all of my dreams, with three kids and a bundle of joy on the way.

I glance down at my left ring finger, where the proof sits. A wave-shaped band adorned with diamonds that fit right over Janey's ring, with a diamond in the middle that looks like it's being lifted by a wave.

After jumping through some hoops, we were able to hire a contractor to combine Sig's and Ada's house into one, complete with a backyard pool, a hot tub, and enough bedrooms for all the kids we plan to have.

I even got the perfect remote job—one that lets me work from a poolside duck or the comfort of home once our newest family member arrives. I love the work, and the Rubber Duckie World brings in so much revenue, I have the freedom to quit whenever I want.

"See, even Rachel agrees." Lisa snaps me out of my thoughts, though I have no recollection of what I just agreed to. "This castle was a waste of time."

"Wait, I didn't—" I start, but Noah interrupts.

"It's not fair!" he cries. "Alien duckie fits through the door. I checked."

And I wish I'd actually read the parenting book propped up on my belly, so I'd know the right thing to say. Or that Sig could talk in duckie form, so he could say it for me.

I'm still at a loss when Anna picks up princess duckie and sets her next to the much larger Duckie Sig. "Toy duckies are smaller than shifter duckies, Noah. See?"

He pouts. "I know that."

Lisa crosses her arms in front of her chest. "Whatever. Let's do something else."

She reminds me so much of her mom. All three kids do. I can almost picture Janey sitting next to them, glaring at the castle right along with them.

"You know..." I say thoughtfully. "Your mom was in a similar situation once."

They forget all about the castle and spin around to face me.

"She was?" Anna asks softly.

I nod. "She'd been working on an essay that was due the next day. A *really* important essay. It was worth half her grade." I'm making up that last part, though I remember how much she was freaking out, so maybe it actually was worth fifty percent. "She was almost finished when the power went out."

Anna gasps. "Was it really dark?"

Noah's eyes widen. "Was Mom *scared*?"

I shake my head. "Not the least bit."

"Mom was super brave," Lisa announces.

"She was." I smile. "And the power came back a few minutes later. But your mom's entire essay was gone."

"Gone?" Lisa gasps.

"All of it?" Anna asks in a small voice.

Even Noah seems invested, and he's definitely not old enough to understand the importance of college essays. He just loves stories about his mom. All three kids do. Heck, they'd probably be just as enraptured by a story about the time Janey spilled coffee on her shirt.

"Your mom didn't give up," I tell them. "She rewrote the entire essay, from scratch."

They stare at me, wide-eyed, waiting.

"And your dad helped, too." It had been right after they started dating, and proof she'd finally met the one. "Every few hours, he would drop by with little gifts."

Noah perks up. "What kind of gifts?"

"Things to help her stay motivated so she could finish that essay. A rose. A poem. A chocolate bar. A bowl of ramen." I chuckle. "She needed sustenance."

"Can we have chocolate?" Noah asks.

Lisa perks up. "We need sustenance, too."

I shake my head. "Not until after dinner."

Noah pouts. "No fair."

"You'd spoil your appetite," Anna tells her siblings.

I smile gratefully at her. "There's a reason I told you kids this story." And, note to self, do not tell stories that involve chocolate. "That essay was just like your castle. You're going to have to redo it. But that's okay. I know you kids are just like your mom. You're dedicated and hard-working, and you never give up!"

They all nod emphatically. Look at me knocking this guardian thing out of the water!

"Did Mom get her paper in on time?" Ana asks.

"I actually can't remember."

"I bet she did," Noah says.

"She definitely did," Lisa says. "Just like we're going to rebuild this castle and make it even better."

"I know you can do it," I tell them, setting aside the parenting book. For now, anyway.

I still miss Janey every day. But the more I talk about her, and the more I share the stories, the less it hurts. Now I can finally smile back at all the wonderful memories we shared. And I can see a part of her in each of her three remarkable kids. Lisa's fiery confidence reminds me of the way Janey would always walk into a room like she owned it. Anna's gentle sweetness is the side Janey saved for those closest to her, and Noah's boundless energy is so like her vibrant spirit.

My heart is full of gratitude for the blessing of having these three kids in my life, each day with them a precious reminder of my best friend.

I wipe away some errant tears—pregnancy really does make you emotional—and listen to the kids debate the best way to rebuild.

They've just agreed to take down the roof when the doorbell rings, and Ada's voice echoes from the kitchen. "Could you get that, Sig? I'm about to take the pie out of the oven."

The only problem is that Sig is in too precarious a position to shift back. If he does, he'll end up on top of the castle, and I'm pretty sure it wasn't built to hold a grown man.

Noah lunges toward him, eyes wide. "He'll crush the castle!"

"Don't shift," Lisa shouts.

Anna jumps to her feet. "We'll get the door," she cries. "I bet it's Reaper. And he might be small enough to fit through the door without a rebuild."

"Good thinking, Sis," Lisa scrambles up after her.

"Oh yeah!" Noah lights up. He drops Sig—who can't get hurt in duckie form—down next to the castle and takes off.

"Wait! Noah, you need to move Sig."

It's like the boy doesn't even hear me.

"Don't shift, I've got this," I tell Sig, then shout, "Girls, grab the stool and check the peephole."

"We will," Lisa yells back. Thank goodness for that.

I push off the couch and waddle toward Sig. "I feel like a duck. And not in a good way."

And there is a good way. Sig's proven that in bed and in the tub, over and over again.

And duck sounds much better than whale, which is a much more accurate description of how I feel... and look. I place my hand on my belly. *Any day now, little one. Any day now.*

"It's Reaper," Lisa shouts from the foyer, distracting me. "He's got food."

My mouth waters, because Sig's best friend's cooking is so good, it puts cruise ship food to shame. And the ships I've worked on hired some of the best chefs.

"I'll be right there," I call out and stare down at duckie Sig. I'd have to squat down to pick him up, and there's a good chance I'd lose my balance and end up destroying the kids' castle in the process. "I'll just send one of the kids to come grab you."

Sig doesn't reply. He can't, since he's in duckie form.

"I'll be quick," I add as I waddle away. Quick-ish.

The delicious smell of Ada's baking wafts into the hallway from the kitchen, and my mouth waters as I join Reaper and the kids.

"Hi, Reap," Noah cries, throwing his arms around the man, who's struggling to balance two large trays above the boy's head.

I'd offer to take them, but I'm not sure I'd manage, either.

"Careful, Noah," Lisa scolds. "Hi, Reaper. We really need your help."

Anna nods. "Sig's too big, but you'll fit."

Reaper sends me a questioning glance, and I decide to leave him guessing. "Noah, can you please go get Sig?"

"Oh yeah." The little boy takes off.

"Come on in, Reap." I give him a quick side-hug so my belly and his food trays don't clash and gesture at the ottoman. "Why don't you set those down there? They smell delicious."

"I'll be right out, Reaper," Ada calls from the kitchen just as Noah runs back in, carrying Duckie Sig. "I'm just finishing up in here."

"No rush, Ada," he calls back. "I made fried chicken, meatloaf, and mac and cheese." Reaper sniffs the air. "Whatever you've got in the oven smells even better."

"You mean this baby?" I glance down at my belly innocently.

Reaper bursts out laughing and so do the twins. Ada chuckles from the kitchen, and I imagine Sig's laughing too—though silently, since rubber ducks can't laugh.

Noah just looks confused. "It's apple pie," he says proudly. "We helped Nana mix the ingredients."

"You did well, kids," Ada calls out. "Can you three set the table? It's almost time for dinner."

"Coming." Lisa takes off, shouting, "Last one there has to fix the roof."

Her siblings run after her.

"Noah! Bring Sig back!" I shout.

"Oh yeah! Sorry, Sig." He sets the rubber duckie in the foyer and then races off after his sisters. "No fair!"

And I'm grinning, because yes, our house is chaotic, but it's also full of life. And that's what I've been missing all along. All the travel, the cruises, the distractions—none of them could fill the hole that losing my best friend left. But being here, with Sig, her kids, and her mom, is exactly what I needed all along.

Sig shifts back with a huge grin. "How's our little bun doing?" he asks as he moves to my side and places his palm against my belly.

It's such an innocent gesture, but feeling his hands on me, anywhere, makes me want his hands on me, *everywhere*.

I snuggle into his side, enjoying the warm, strong feel of him. "Our little bun is thinking it's time to be born," I say hopefully.

Ada pops out of the kitchen, a towel in her hands. "It's good to see you, Reaper. Come on in. I'm dying to hear about that neighbor of yours."

Reaper shoots an accusatory glance at Sig. "What have you been telling her, Duckie?"

Sig raises his hands up in surrender. "Hey, it wasn't me. I only told Rachel, and you know I don't keep anything from her."

"Fair enough," Reaper grumbles, his gaze turning to me.

"I may have said something," I tell him. "But only because I know you like her."

Reaper's cheeks flush scarlet. "I do not. She's pregnant with another man's baby."

"A man who's not in the picture."

This time, Reaper bunches his hands into fists. "How does a man leave his woman and child behind?"

"He's no man, that's how," Ada says, and she's absolutely right.

Reaper shrugs. "Maybe they'll get together."

Sig nudges my shoulder lightly, as if to say, *I'm not buying his nonchalance, are you?* I nudge him back to tell him *I am so not.*

"Why don't you invite her to dinner anyway?" I suggest.

He scowls. "I don't even know her."

"You could *get* to know her," Sig says.

Reaper's scowl deepens. "Who says I even like her?"

"You like her," we all chorus. Even the kids, who pop their heads out of the dining room.

"You want to kiss her," Lisa adds in a sing-song voice.

Anna giggles.

Noah makes a gagging sound.

Sig and I exchange a smile.

Ada pats his shoulder. "It's never a good idea to lie to yourself."

"The only reason I mentioned her," Reaper snaps, "is because she's pregnant like Rachel. That's it!"

"Right..." I say.

"We believe you, man," Sig adds. His tone says anything but.

Reaper turns a little red, spins around, and grabs the food trays. "I'll take these to the dining room!"

He storms off, Ada and the kids on his heels, leaving me and Sig in the foyer.

I grin. "We should really stop teasing him, shouldn't we?"

Sig pouts. "But it's so much fun."

I giggle, since I know he truly cares for his friend and is just teasing, and then grimace when the baby kicks.

"Do you need to sit down?" Sig asks softly.

I nod. "I could really use a break from being pregnant. Carry me to the living room?"

And then I shift. Thankfully not into a giant cruise ship, or even a tiny one. I shift into a wave-shaped gold ring with diamonds.

And I marvel at how lucky I am to be here, in this moment, with Sig and our family.

***

Thank you for reading RUBBER DUCKIE SHIFTER NEXT DOOR. Reaper's story, HOT PEPPER SHIFTER NEXT DOOR, is coming soon!

If you enjoyed Rachel and Sig's story, you're going to love HER PASTRY SHIFTERS! A curvy baker accidentally ends up sharing a hotel room with three hot men who shift into pastries. **One-click to read HER PASTRY SHIFTERS by Mia Harlan today.**

Looking for more unique shifters with plenty of spice?

- I've got some delicious men who shift into donuts in HER DONUT SHIFTERS BY MIA HARLAN. *I hate donuts. Can three donut shifters change my mind?*

- Amber can shift into anyone she meets, and one of her fated mates Chase, is a bunny shifter who knows how to use his carrot in AMBER BY MIA HALRAN. *I'm in love with my best friend. But one sip of a spelled latte, and two shifters are calling me their mate.*

- Violet is a 20-year-old in an 80-year-old's body in VIOLET BY MIA HARLAN. *My chameleon shifter powers let me take the shape of anyone I want... and I've spent the past year posing as my 80-year-old best friend!*

- Wynter's mate Xavi shifts into a block of ice and her other mate Leith can shift into anyone he meets in WYNTER BY MIA HARLAN *I'm Zoe Wynter, the best magical maid in town, and rumor has it I'm about to go to jail.*

If you enjoyed this book, I would really appreciate it if you could share it or leave a review. Word of mouth is how other readers find my books, and that's what allows me continue doing what I love: writing!

About Mia Harlan

Mia is a USA Today & International Bestselling Author who writes quirky romance guaranteed to make you laugh.

A librarian by day and author by night, she lives in Canada with her husband (who's definitely NOT a vampire) and their Mini Mortal (who doesn't have fangs).

For more exclusive content, visit miaharlan.com

Also By Mia Harlan

Shifter Bay

Enter a world like no other, and fall in love at first sight with unique, quirky object shifters.

Her Donut Shifters

Her Pastry Shifters

Rubber Duckie Shifter Next Door

Hot Pepper Shifter Next Door (coming soon)

Silver Springs

Lose yourself in a quirky, paranormal small town filled with magic and fated mates.

Amber

Amber: Deja Brew

Amber Goes Yeti

Amber's Christmas Surprise

Violet

Deflated (with Eva Delaney)

Violet: A Monster-ly Undercover Christmas

Wynter

Minnie

Moonlit Nephrite (with Eva Delaney)

Tall, Dark, and Haunted (with Hanleigh Bradley)

Saturn (with Hanleigh Bradley)

Venus (with Hanleigh Bradley)

Neptune (with Hanleigh Bradley)

Beach Romance (Writing as Mia Sands)

Librarians find love at a beach resort in these spicy shorts.

Mile High Librarian

Mister Fit

Other

An Espresso Machine's Guide to Love and Mischief (with Eva Delaney)

Glow Sticks (with Sapphire Winters)

Paranormal Reverse Harem Romance Reader
Challenge: A Coloring Book